JR. CHAPTER BOOK

THE
BAILEY SCHOOL
KIDS

JR. CHAPTER BOOK

THE BAILEY SCHOOL KIDS®

PIRATES DO RIDE SCOOTERS

by Marcia Thornton Jones and Debbie Dadey
Illustrated by Joëlle Dreidemy

SCHOLASTIC INC.
New York Toronto London Auckland Sydney
Mexico City New Delhi Hong Kong Buenos Aires

To Thelma Kuhljuergen Thornton—
the best Mom in the world who made sure I learned to
swim and who was never EVER late!—M.T.J.

To my Allen County relatives—
Seth and Sam Kitches, and Matthew Holder—
thanks for reading my books—D.D.

To my buddy Adrien, alias Billy Guitar,
the greatest pirate of Brittany!—J.D.

ISBN-10: 0-439-87632-X
ISBN-13: 978-0-439-87632-2

12 11 10 9 8 7   12 13/0

Printed in the U.S.A.
First printing, April 2007

CONTENTS

1

VROOM!

Liza, Melody, Howie, and Eddie stopped in front of the gate to the pool. "Too early!" Eddie yelled. "This is terrible." A big lock hung on the gate.

"I can't wait to practice water polo," Melody said.

"Practice?" Eddie said. "That sounds like work."

"It will be fun," Melody said. "You can really slam the ball."

 Eddie thought about slamming the ball over the net.

He dreamed of sending it clear to the moon.

"Maybe it will be fun," Eddie said.

Eddie waved his water noodle through the air. "I am ready for a summer full of splashing fun," he said. By accident, he bopped Liza on the head with the noodle. He poked Melody in the back. He smacked Howie's books out of his arms. (Howie loved to read. Even when he didn't have to.)

Liza grabbed the noodle before Eddie could swat her again. "Stop," she told him. "You'll pop my float."

Lots more people joined the kids at the gate. Tall people. Short people. Big people and small people.

Everyone wanted to get into the cool water. Suddenly, they all heard a loud noise.

Vrrroooooom!

A scooter roared into the parking lot.

The scooter zoomed toward the pool.

The scooter squealed to a stop beside Melody, Liza, Howie, and Eddie. It was bright red with a big skeleton between the handlebars.

A very tall woman hopped off. She took off her helmet and hung it on the handlebars. A black bandana covered most of her head. Long curly red hair popped out below it.

She pulled a key from the pocket of her leather jacket and looked at her watch. *"Arrrrrgh!"* she said as she unlocked the gate. "I'm late! Out of me way!"

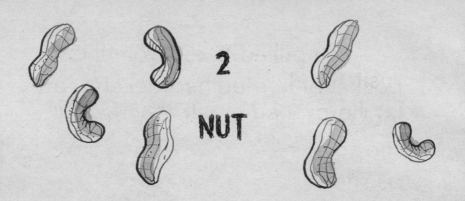

2
NUT

"I'm Last Minute Molly and I'm the boss of this here ship," the lady barked as people streamed past her and through the pool gate.

"Ship?" Eddie asked. "What ship?" He waved his water noodle. It came very close to bopping Molly on the head.

"No monkey business," Molly said as she pushed the wild noodle out of her way. "Or you'll be walking the plank."

Eddie grumbled, "What kind of nut is she?"

"She's no nut," Howie told his friends. "She must be the lifeguard. Lifeguards keep things safe. They don't allow running. They don't put up with silliness. And they don't allow fighting. Lifeguards have to be serious."

15

"Well, she looks like a nut to me," Eddie said.

Molly did look a little different. When she took off her jacket, they saw that she was wearing a striped bathing suit that hung to her knees!

Just then, Last Minute Molly stood at the edge of the pool and yelled, "SHARK!"

SHARK!

3

SHARK

Kids ran
left. Kids ran
right. Kids
smacked into
each other.
Last
Minute Molly
stopped them
all by blowing on a whistle.

"That whistle sounded like a parrot," Melody said, but none of her friends were listening to her. They were looking in the pool for a shark.

"We should get help," Liza whimpered. "Call a Shark Fighter!"

"Bwa-ha-ha!" Last Minute Molly laughed so hard tears trickled down her cheeks.

"You landlubbers are just too much! There be no real sharks lurking in this pool."

"But you yelled 'shark'," Howie told her.

"That I did," Molly said, looking at Eddie's noodle. "It's time for a little water game. Not all are lucky enough to have pool toys. We want fun for one and all!"

"Game? Count me in," Eddie said as he pushed aside a few kids.

"Then listen to me rules for the game of Shark," Molly said.

"Rules? Rules? I don't need rules!" Eddie said.

Molly looked Eddie square
in the eye. "On my ship, there
be rules," she said. "Now listen
up, matey, or you'll be walking
the plank!"

The rest of the kids listened while Molly told them how to play. "One person is the shark. The others swim from one side of the pool to the other. If the shark tags you, you become a shark, too. The last person to escape the touch of the sharks is the winner."

The kids jumped in the pool to play. Everyone except Liza. She stood on the edge, clutching her float.

"Hop on in," Molly told her. "The water is fine."

"I...I...I can't swim," Liza told her.

Molly scratched under her bandana. "Not to worry. You can make sure they follow me."

Eddie didn't like rules. He just wanted the game to start. He pushed past Liza and jumped into the pool.

Liza teetered on the edge of the pool. She tottered. She started to fall.

HELP!

4

WALKING THE PLANK

Molly grabbed Liza around the waist just before she ker-plunked into the deep end.

"Sorry," Eddie told Liza.

Molly pointed to Liza. "You should learn to swim. I can teach you." Then Molly pointed to Eddie. "You," she said, "will be walking the plank!"

Molly led Eddie to the diving area. The rest of the kids followed. Everyone wanted to see Eddie walk the plank.

"Walk the plank?" Melody said. "That sounds bad. Very bad."

At the diving board, Molly stopped. She whispered into Eddie's ear.

Eddie walked toward the end of the board.

"Time out?" he cried. "I can't be given a time out. I just got here." Eddie groaned. He frowned. He whacked his noodle against the diving board.

BAM
BAM

Liza waved to Eddie from
the shallow end.

"Watch this," Melody called
to Eddie. She tossed her ball
high into the air and caught it.

Howie tried to cheer up
Eddie. "Do you want to look
at one of my books?" Howie
asked.

Eddie shook his head.
He wanted to play in the pool,
and he wanted to play now.
He slapped his noodle on the
surface of the water. Eddie
smiled and dipped the long
purple toy into the pool. He
blew on the other end of
the tube.

SQUIRT!
Water flew all over the
pool.

SQUIRT!
Water blasted onto Howie's
books.

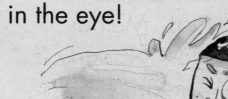

SQUIRT!
Water zapped Molly right
in the eye!

31

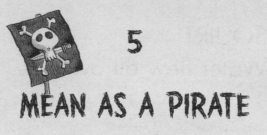

5
MEAN AS A PIRATE

The kids stood outside the pool the next morning, waiting for it to open.

"Last Minute Molly is mean," Eddie said. "She's meaner than the school secretary without her coffee!"

"No!" Melody gasped. "Nobody is THAT mean!"

"She's even meaner than a pirate without a treasure," Eddie added.

"Molly isn't mean at all," Liza said. "She saved me from falling into the deep end of the pool. She said she would teach me to swim."

Melody bounced her ball off of Eddie's red hair.

"She told me she would teach us how to play water polo."

BUMP

A loud noise made Melody drop her ball.

Vrrroooooom!
VRRROOOOOOOOOM!
SCRREEEEEEEEEEECH!

Last Minute Molly squealed to a stop next to Melody, Liza, Howie, and Eddie. The lifeguard hopped off her scooter. Molly pulled off her helmet and hung it on the handle bars.

That's when Melody gasped.

6

SMUGGLED TREASURES

"Are you okay?" Liza asked.

"Do you have a fever?" Howie asked.

"Did you swallow a bug?" Eddie wanted to know.

Melody pointed a trembling finger as Molly rushed to the gate. "It's not a bug. It's HER!"

"Same scooter," Eddie said. "Same silly swimsuit. Same crazy hair."

Then Molly looked over her shoulder. That's when the kids saw the big, black patch.

"Eddie," Howie whispered, "you DID hurt her eye."

"I didn't mean to," Eddie told his friends.

All the kids went up to the pool gate, but Molly held up a hand.

"Bwa-ha-ha," she laughed. "Not so fast, me little fishes. Before you get in the water. I'll be a-looking through those beachy bags."

Bwahaha

"Why?" asked a kid with a soccer ball peeking out from his bag.

"I'm looking for contraband," Molly said.

"Con-tra-band?" a girl repeated. "Is that a music group?"

"Is it something you put on a cut?" someone else asked.

"I think it's stretchy rubber you put around papers," another kid said.

Last Minute Molly peered down at the kids with her one good eye. "Contraband is smuggled treasures," she told them. "I plan to teach you a little bit about one for all and all for one! Now open those bags or you'll be walking me plank!"

BAILEY CITY POOL
HOURS
10:00 - 7:00

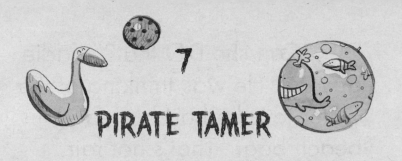

7
PIRATE TAMER

Molly peeked in each kid's bag. She plucked out all the water toys. She pulled out balls and bats. She snatched dolls.

"Can she DO that?" Eddie gasped. He was thinking of the water toys he had buried in his beach bag. "That's not fair."

Melody pulled her friends away from Molly and closer to the pool. "Eddie is right," she told them.

"What are you talking about?" Liza asked Melody. "Eddie is never right."

"He is this time," Melody said, "because Last Minute Molly isn't a normal lifeguard. I think she's a pirate!"

"A pirate?" yelped Liza as she backed farther away from Molly. Melody grabbed Liza before she tumbled into a garbage can.

SHE'S A PIRATE!

A PIRATE???

Eddie pretended his noodle was a sword and gave it a big swing through the air. "Look out! I'm Sir Edward, the Pirate Tamer."

RRDARR

"You can't tame a pirate," Howie said quietly.

"Why not?" Eddie asked.

"Because pirates aren't real. They are just in books. They don't live in Bailey City and they definitely don't ride scooters," Howie said.

"Pirates DO ride scooters. At least this one does," Melody said. "But if it's proof you need, then it's proof you'll get."

"What kind of proof?" Liza asked.

"Meet me here at dusk, and you'll see," Melody said.

8

HOT ON THE PIRATE TRAIL

"This is a dumb idea," Eddie said. "I would rather be eating ice cream, catching bugs, or playing videao games."

Eddie and his three friends stood behind the pool trash cans with their bikes. They were waiting for Last Minute Molly to leave the pool.

"I'm going to prove that we have a pirate problem," Melody told Liza, Eddie, and Howie.

Finally, Last Minute Molly locked the gates. She had a giant bag over her shoulder.

"She has our treasures," Howie whispered. Molly put on her helmet and climbed on her scooter.

Luckily, Last Minute Molly couldn't go very fast because of the big bag. Melody, Liza, Eddie and Howie hopped on their bikes and were hot on her trail.

They pedaled up hills.

They pedaled down hills.

They rode, and rode, and rode some more.

Finally, Last Minute Molly parked in front of a house on the Red River.

The kids darted behind a tree.

They hid behind bushes.

They followed Molly around to the back of the house.

Eddie blinked his eyes to
get a better look.
Liza gasped.
Howie slapped his cheeks.
"I told you so," Melody
said.

9
MUTINY

A boat was tied to a dock behind the house. This wasn't just any boat. It was a ship.

"Aaack! Molly late! Molly late!" a parrot screeched.

AAACK!

Molly tossed the sack on the deck. The parrot hopped on her shoulder and pecked at Molly's ear.

"It won't be long, me pretty," Molly told the bird.

"Not long! Not long!" the parrot repeated as they went into the house, leaving the treasure on the ship.

Not long!

"Now do you believe me?" Melody asked her friends.

"Molly looks like a pirate.  She acts like a pirate. She even has a ship and a parrot.

Last Minute Molly IS a
pirate! And she won't stop
until she has all of our summer
treasures."

"No!" gasped Eddie.
"We can't let that happen."

"Exactly," Melody said.
"Follow me!"

Melody led her three
friends onto the ship.

They found the bag full of summer toys. Melody found her ball. Howie found his books. Eddie found his noodle. Liza found her float.

Just then, the kids heard a terrible sound. Molly and the parrot were after them. "AAAAAACK! Mutiny on board! Mutiny on board!"

10
SPLASH!

Melody screamed as the parrot swooped over her head. Howie ducked.

Eddie swung at the bird
with his noodle. He missed, but
he did hit Liza's back.

Liza's feet slipped. She
grabbed for the rail. But she
missed.

Whoosh!

Splash!

Ker-plunk!

Liza fell right into the
Red River.

"HELP! Liza can't swim!" screamed Melody.

"AAACCKKK!" screeched the parrot.

"AHHHHHHH!" screamed Howie and Eddie.

Suddenly,
last Minute
Molly dove
into the river.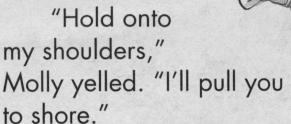
"Hold onto
my shoulders,"
Molly yelled. "I'll pull you
to shore."

Eddie, Melody, and Howie
waited on dry land for Molly
and Liza. Molly placed Liza on
the shore and headed toward
her scooter. "Why did you take
all of our treasures?" called
Howie.

"You can't get away with
this," Melody shouted. "We
know you are a pirate."

"We'll tell the police,"
Howie told her.

"AAAAACK! Police!
Police!" the bird squawked.

"Aaarrrgh," Molly said
as she climbed onto her scooter.
"This isn't the end of Last Minute
Molly. I'll be back!"

Her parrot soared away
from the boat and landed on her
helmet. Together, they zoomed
away.

"We did it," Melody said. "We saved Bailey City from a toy-stealing pirate."

"I'm not so sure," Liza said. She pointed to a sign on the side of the boat. "Could it be that Last Minute Molly isn't really a pirate? After all, she did save my life."

Melody, Howie, and Eddie stared at the sign. "She looked like a pirate," Howie said.

"She acted like a pirate," Eddie added.

"I have some toys I could donate to the toy drive," Liza said.

Melody nodded. "I do, too."

"Let's just hope we're safe from pirates once and for all," Eddie said.

"Never," Howie said. "Not as long as we're in Bailey City!"